Autumn
Publishing

Published in 2018
by Autumn Publishing
Cottage Farm
Sywell
NN6 0BJ
www.igloobooks.com

LEO002 0418
2 4 6 8 10 9 7 5 3 1
ISBN 978-1-78810-239-1

Printed and manufactured in China

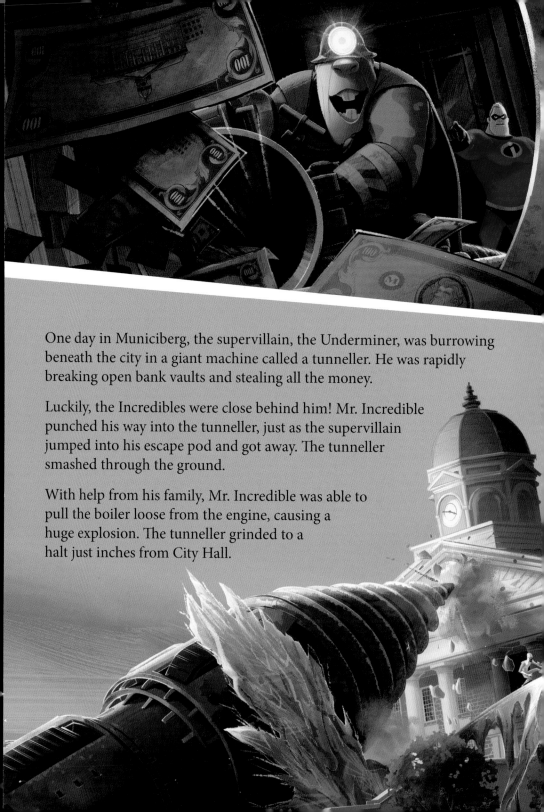

One day in Municiberg, the supervillain, the Underminer, was burrowing beneath the city in a giant machine called a tunneller. He was rapidly breaking open bank vaults and stealing all the money.

Luckily, the Incredibles were close behind him! Mr. Incredible punched his way into the tunneller, just as the supervillain jumped into his escape pod and got away. The tunneller smashed through the ground.

With help from his family, Mr. Incredible was able to pull the boiler loose from the engine, causing a huge explosion. The tunneller grinded to a halt just inches from City Hall.

The family was surrounded by police and blamed for the destruction of the city. "You would have preferred we did nothing?" asked Mr. Incredible.

"Without a doubt," replied a government official, who swiftly reminded him superheroes were illegal.

Back at the motel the family were discussing their future as Supers.

"Superheroes are illegal," said Helen. "Whether it's fair or not, that's the law."

However, later that night, Lucius Best, also known as Frozone, informed the family that a business tycoon wanted to make Supers legal and needed their help.

That same night, Mr. Incredible, Elastigirl and Frozone arrived at a massive company called DevTech, which was owned by Winston Deavor, and his sister, Evelyn. Winston blamed the death of their parents on the absence of Supers.

Winston wanted the public to see the Supers in action, and techy Evelyn showed them a small camera for their supersuits that would record their heroic acts. It was then announced that the first mission would go to Elastigirl.

Back at the motel, Helen was reluctant to accept the job, but with her husband's support, she accepted Winston's offer.

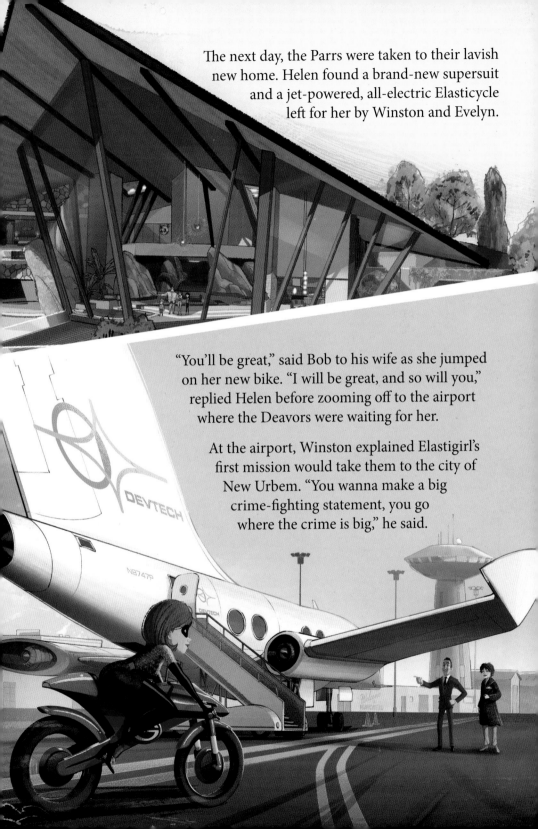

The next day, the Parrs were taken to their lavish new home. Helen found a brand-new supersuit and a jet-powered, all-electric Elasticycle left for her by Winston and Evelyn.

"You'll be great," said Bob to his wife as she jumped on her new bike. "I will be great, and so will you," replied Helen before zooming off to the airport where the Deavors were waiting for her.

At the airport, Winston explained Elastigirl's first mission would take them to the city of New Urbem. "You wanna make a big crime-fighting statement, you go where the crime is big," he said.

The following morning, Bob explained to Violet and Dash that their mum had left for a new job. This didn't make sense to Violet. "So, Mum is going out, illegally, to explain why she shouldn't be illegal?" Bob wasn't sure how to answer, but luckily for him, the school bus arrived.

Meanwhile, in New Urbem, Elastigirl was trying to stop a runaway hovertrain! Driving as fast as she could through tunnels and across roofs on the Elasticycle, Elastigirl finally caught up with the train. She grabbed the carriage and stretched into a giant parachute to slow the train down. It stopped just seconds from disaster!

Elastigirl was checking all the passengers were okay, when she noticed a message appear on the train's control panel.
It said: *Welcome back, Elastigirl – The Screenslaver.*

Back at home, Bob started to read a bedtime story to Jack-Jack, but the baby dozed off. Feeling exhausted and missing his wife, it didn't take long for Bob to fall asleep on the sofa.

A short while later, Jack-Jack woke up to a noise outside. Looking out of the door, he spotted a raccoon stealing food from the bins. With its black-mask face it looked like a burglar. The baby ran towards the glass door... and passed straight through it! Jack-Jack was no ordinary baby, he had super powers like the rest of his family! Determined to stop the furry criminal, the Super baby burst into flames and chased the startled raccoon across the garden.

Suddenly, a loud CRASH woke Bob and he saw Jack-Jack firing laser beams from his eyes towards the terrified animal. It was chaos, and when Bob tried to intervene, Jack-Jack multiplied into five babies!

"You have powers!" shouted Bob. "Yeah, baby!" But his excitement quickly vanished. If his youngest son had multiple powers, Bob had a big problem.

Meanwhile, Elastigirl was being interviewed about her train rescue, when suddenly a hypnotic pattern appeared on every screen, and the host, Chad Brentley, said in a robotic voice: "Screens are everywhere. We are controlled by screens. And screens are controlled by me, the Screenslaver!"

The Screenslaver then threatened to crash the ambassador's helicopter, so Elastigirl sprang into action. She jumped out of the window and stretched to reach the rooftop.

Spotting the helicopter flying above the city, Elastigirl leapt inside it and found the pilots in a trance. She quickly smashed the screens to break the hypnosis, and then rescued the ambassador and everyone on-board just as the chopper flew out of control. Elastigirl had saved the day once again!

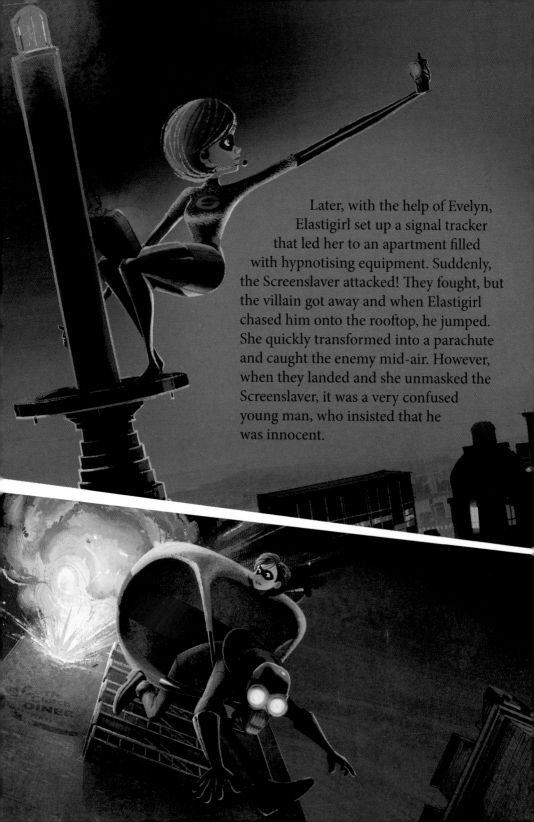

Later, with the help of Evelyn, Elastigirl set up a signal tracker that led her to an apartment filled with hypnotising equipment. Suddenly, the Screenslaver attacked! They fought, but the villain got away and when Elastigirl chased him onto the rooftop, he jumped. She quickly transformed into a parachute and caught the enemy mid-air. However, when they landed and she unmasked the Screenslaver, it was a very confused young man, who insisted that he was innocent.

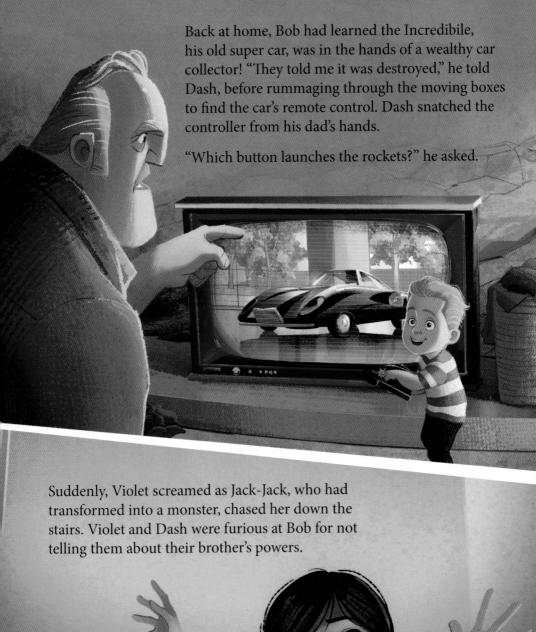

Back at home, Bob had learned the Incredibile, his old super car, was in the hands of a wealthy car collector! "They told me it was destroyed," he told Dash, before rummaging through the moving boxes to find the car's remote control. Dash snatched the controller from his dad's hands.

"Which button launches the rockets?" he asked.

Suddenly, Violet screamed as Jack-Jack, who had transformed into a monster, chased her down the stairs. Violet and Dash were furious at Bob for not telling them about their brother's powers.

The following day, leaders and Supers gathered in the DevTech penthouse, as there would be a summit on Winston's yacht later. Elastigirl and Evelyn were in the editing room, examining the footage of the Screenslaver's lair from her suit cameras. Something didn't feel right. "Look," said Elastigirl. "One of the Screenslaver's monitors was tuned into my suit cam. Isn't the suit cam closed circuit?"

"Maybe he hacked it," said Evelyn, shrugging.

Elastigirl still felt uneasy. "All the Screenslaver needs to do to hypnotise someone is get a screen in front of their eyes," she realised. "But what if the screen doesn't look like a screen?" Elastigirl picked up the hypno-goggles and looked at them closely. Small screens were built into the lenses! Suddenly, Evelyn forced the goggles onto Elastigirl and bright, hypnotic lights flashed. Elastigirl was in a trance.

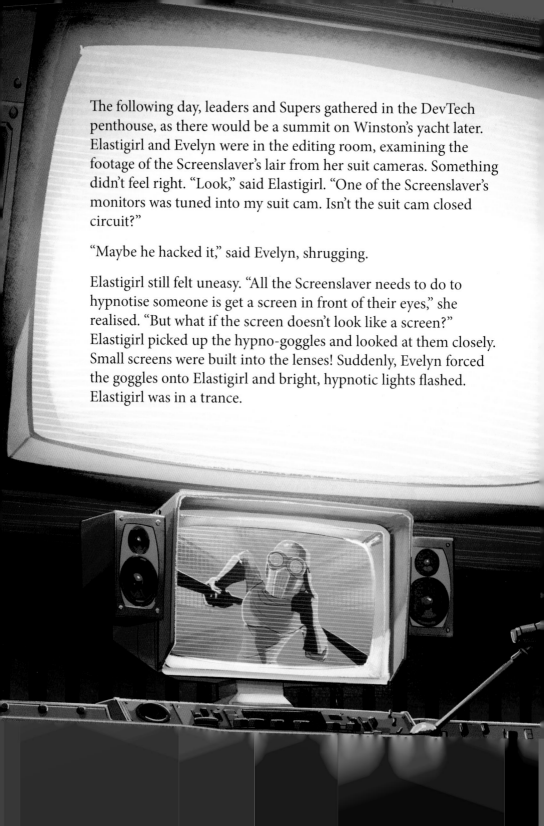

Elastigirl woke a while later and found herself in a freezing room. If she tried to stretch she would surely break. "So you're the Screenslaver," said Elastigirl to Evelyn, who was glaring at her from the other side of a glass wall. "Why would you betray your brother?"

Evelyn smiled. "Superheroes keep us weak," she explained.

"Are you going to kill me?" asked Elastigirl. Evelyn smirked cruelly. "Nah, using you is better. You're going to help me make Supers illegal forever." With that, she placed Elastigirl back under hypnosis.

Back at the Parr family home, the phone rang. It was Evelyn. "Elastigirl's in trouble," she said. "Meet me on the ship." Bob quickly called Lucius to watch the kids while he went to save his wife.

Soon after Bob left, six hypnotised Supers appeared at the house to take the kids! Frozone arrived just in time and created a giant wall of ice to protect them, but it didn't take long for the Supers to break down the wall. As the fight continued, the Incredibile suddenly burst into the living room! Dash had summoned it using the remote control. The kids escaped in the vehicle just as the Supers captured Frozone and put a pair of hypno-goggles over his eyes.

Later, as agreed, Mr. Incredible met Evelyn on the yacht. Suddenly, wearing the hypno-goggles, Elastigirl pounced on him. "Helen, it's me!" he cried, as his wife put a pair of goggles over his eyes. Mr. Incredible fell silent and still.

On board his ship, Winston
welcomed his guests and declared the signing ceremony was about to begin.
"I thank all of you for representing your nation's commitment to superheroes,"
he said. However, during a group photo, Evelyn hypnotised everyone and
ordered the Supers to speed up the yacht and destroy the controls.
The ship was on course to crash into the city!

Meanwhile, the kids knew their parents were in trouble, so they sped off in the Incredibile to save them. They boarded the yacht and burst into the conference room. Jack-Jack removed Elastigirl's goggles, who then quickly snatched Mr. Incredible's and Frozone's off, too. Evelyn was watching from the control room and ordered the Supers to attack, but one-by-one, The Incredibles and Frozone removed the Supers' hypno-goggles. Before long, everyone was released from Evelyn's control.

The other Supers needed to turn the yacht to stop it crashing into the city. Mr. Incredible had to get to the rudder. He tied himself to the anchor and went underwater. Using all his strength, he moved the rudder and the ship began to turn.

Meanwhile, Evelyn tried to escape in a jet, but Elastigirl entered the cockpit just as the plane took off. "You will never become legal… ever!" taunted Evelyn. As the jet flew higher and higher, Elastigirl was struggling to breathe, so she grabbed a flare gun and shot it at Evelyn's oxygen tank, which ruptured and hurled the villain through the windshield.

Elastigirl jumped after her and before they hit the ocean below, Voyd, one of the Supers, created a portal that allowed them to land on the deck of the yacht, just before it came to a grinding halt in front of the city. Finally, the real Screenslaver was arrested and the city was saved!

The public were very grateful to the Supers and, once again, they were recognised as heroes. A judge thanked them for their extraordinary service and restored their legal status! Driving along in the Incredi-Wagon, the Incredibles were ready to take on anything that came their way – and they would do so together, as a family.